Poems
& Stories

KATRINA McKEOWN

First published 2020
ISBN: 9798620731749

An Inherit The Earth Publication ©2020 In conjunction
with Amazon.

Editor's Preface.

I got to know about Katrina through a friend of mine called Lorna Kerr. Lorna told me about Katrina's writing and put her in touch with me. Together we formulated a plan to get Katrina's unique style of writing published. This is Katrina's first published book. She has been writing for over 20 years now. Hopefully this is the first of many publications from her. Enjoy her poems and short stories. I know I did.

Meek
March 2020.

For

Shirley,

x

Contents –

Poems Part I

The Moon
The Rain
Bonnie Lass
Endure
Learn To Live Again
Let's All Gather By The Shore
Mystical Tour
I'm Lost
Love's Shower
Down With Love
Love's A Battlefield
Darkness Consumes Me
Material Girls
Winter's Snow
Angel
My Darkness
Christmas Time
Different Strokes For Different Folks
It's About Time
Dancing With Wolves
Writer's Block
Perception Ain't Perfection
Elvis Aaron Presley

Stories Part II

Mermaids
Dog Tales – Star
Realm Of Shadows
A Thrilling Time

PART I

Poems

The Moon.

My brain befell a numb delight from the meds I took
tonight,
The moon sang a song of enticement beneath her breath

Come come come with me, I'll lead the way through
history,
to where love first began and the brotherhood of man,
then we'll come back to our own time and land

Come come come with me, watch you don't get caught in
Space Oddity,
looking down at the Auroras and Cosmic Rays,
up through the Karman line, and Spectacular Galaxies

You'll feel weightless in the Magnitude, it'll give you a
funny attitude,
watch out for the deleterious effects

While we pay an interstellar visit onto Venus, Jupiter and
Mars
making up Cosmic Avatars, now that would be
Spectacular.
Then we'll float gradually back down through the Milky
Way
eating candy floss while relaxing on Clouds, floating past
the stars

I'm your Lonestar navigating you

When you feel the wind on your face, see the clouds in the
sky and watch a bird flap its wings in flight, you're
experiencing the troposphere and it's a pretty nice layer to
call home

The moon sings a song beneath her breath, with what little of the night is left, I'm navigating you back home to bed into a dreamy slumber, away from the cold night air, I'll bid you goodnight.

What a dream I had, I chilled with the moon that night.

The Rain.

Blame my insomniac brain,
for creating a rhythm from the rain, as it forms beats off
my window pane

I would never usually complain about the pitter patter,
spitter spatter but it's showing no restrain.

My brain needs to re train,
itself not to engage with the rain,
so I can re-programme myself to get to sleep while some
night-time still remains

I'll retreat to my comfy cosy bed,
and say goodnight and hope for the best

that sleep will come and let me rest from those
drums beating in my head.

Bonnie Lass.

O' Bonne, Bonnie lass
Yer growing up so fast,

O'er the years I've watched ye grow
Kind and gentle always good,
On occasions jokingly rude,
from a baby very small now ye grown o' so tall,

You've grown in brightness through the years and learned
to cope with tiny fears.

Kind and gentle helpful too, are all the wonders inside
you.

O' Bonnie Bonnie lass
Yer luv for him does show,

O' Bonnie Bonnie lass
for yer luv to grow
You'll have to let him know,

Cause if ye dinny lass
his love you'll never know.

Endure.

I endure as the hours accrue,
I wonder how I will make it through
this non-existent existence.

I'm wearing my mask of resistance,
it has become my worn out disguise,

I can't even remember being without it.
It has clung to my side as it helps me to hide
The truth behind my eyes;
will it ever have the insight to apologise.

As it's taken from me all the truth that's within,
I wouldn't know truth or where to begin,
It was so long ago that the story began,
That's when out the door my feelings they ran
Now it has had a long journey behold of my soul
Mask of masks it's time to let go.

Learn To Live Again.

Through pain and depression,
in the dark clouds above.
Please send me some kindness
and show me some love.

Envisioning water washing it all
away, all the Negativity,
the Sadness,
Anxiety, Depression,
Anger and Regret.
No more of my time
will you ruin do not fret,
letting it all go down the drain.
Will I learn to live again.

Calming my nerves and soothing my brain,
healing me from all forms of pain
Will I learn to live again?

Let's All Gather By The Shore.

Imagine if you can lots of boys and lots of girls in the 50s
music world,
gathering by the shore, to discuss the night before,
the concert they had just been to and what they had seen,
as part of the 50s music scene,
where spirits were raised and different groups were
praised,

Where one for all and all for one they gathered as a team
for what they all believed in,
to have danced and sung to have lived out their wildest
dreams and to feel they are part of the greatest of music
arts.

In times to come to reminiscence upon those days.

Mystical Tour.

A mystical tour is what we are all caught up in,
in this world trying to succeed like a rock band.

Traveling here or there or anywhere
Trying to capture fortune and fame
Sometimes though too easily we give up or get stuck in the
same rut,
Never give up as we all go through periods of bad luck.

Everyone has feelings and finds a way to express their love
joy, tears and tenderness.

Through listening to a famous song by a band and that
band has written the best song it can.
People's feelings have been let out, that's when they start
to sing dance shout and let it all out.

We should make a stand for ourselves and go and find
what it is we need, in our own minds to succeed.

A Mystical Tour is what we're all caught up in, we can all
try our best, and this Mystical Tour will do the rest.

I'm Lost.

My wordsmith brain had been keeping me awake,
I turned it off for a while and it took it as permanently by
mistake,
Now and then I pop on here and read some poems of my
friends,
hoping it might ignite and spark my poetry's creative heart,
but to no avail. It seems to have taken the huff which
means I can't write stuff.
As of yet still nothing is being created in the imagination of
my mind to help me write a rhyme, maybe I just need to
give my imagination more time.

Love's Shower.

We can create a music symphony
With the music from the beats of our hearts
A tender musical harp playing,
forming loving parts.
A rhapsody of romance
to skip a beat and dance,
to print to memory.
Every second chance.
Every second, every minute, every hour.
While love rains down upon us
and we're soaking in its shower.

Down With Love.

Looking around me and the people I see are in and outta
love,
being used or abused, condemned or accused in the
wrong,
in and outta love like some sorta curse

Please keep it away from me, I don't want to catch this
contagious disease
Neurotic life games being played, deliberately pushing
insanity to the edge
and over

I enjoy my peace and quiet, my calm demeanour do not
disturb
My gentle pace in this human race, I'm in no hurry to
finish

I want no part in playing with cupids bow in arrow
it only appears to start great and end in sorrow
in and outta love, I don't need that stuff

Down, down, down with Love

Love's battlefield.

They Fought For her Love

Strike to the Heart a deep damaging blow
as they fought with swords of tempered steel,
blood like raindrops was all they could feel.

He'd been struck by his savage opponent,
his crimson blood mixed into the rain which fell fierce.
Victoriously he struck his attacker with a passionate rage
until his opponent suffering enough flew from the stage

He'd fought in loves own battlefield
A tormented soul making an eternal cry of passion
For the woman he yearned

The lady in question was watching stirring with concern,
Her heart full of passion
Adrenaline pumping through her veins

Captivated by his refined demeanour,
Her cleavage breathless in his victory.
He was pale and so serious

Enticing and inviting she drew him into her web of ecstasy
In a morbid calling bursting forth, he accepted in a
subdued recklessness

With touches of raging passion, lustfully they continued
while inhaling each other's essence
Losing control, in hearts that surrendered
They needed to fall.

Savage nights now devour the hours away
as they devour each other

Before any insecurities take hold

Both of them knowing Love's a Battlefield.

Darkness Consumes Me.

As Darkness Consumes Me, There's No Turning Back,
It's a Journey to Hell Now That's Where I Belong,
As My Soul Burdens Heavily with Wrongs That Have
Come,
There's No Turning Back or Button Undone.

Dressed All in Black Clothing with Crimson Black Hair,
If You Dare to Look My Way, I'll Give You That Stare,
Expressionless Features Now Rest on My Face,
And My Shirt Dons A Collar Made Out of Lace.

With Cuts on My Arms Trying to Let My Pain Out,
Inside I'm Screaming and Can't Get It Out,
To Hide in The Shadows with Others Like Me,
It's A Cope Mechanism from Life and The Pain It May
Bring.

Death Becomes Her Some Might Say
As My Make Up Grimly Hides My Face,
I wouldn't Harm Others Unless They Harm Me,
It's My Cope Mechanism and Others Like Me.

I Respect Death Just as Much as I Do Life,
My Life's Been Overcomplicated, Overrated, Debated
Degraded,
Don't Judge Me cause I Value Death,
It's My Life, Don't Try to Walk in My Shoes,
I Have Intellect and So Do My Friends,
We Share Common Interests in Which by We Are Bound,
We Love and Cherish All of Which We Do Care,
There's No Bad Intentions,
Just A Deep Depression That's Sometimes Hard to Bear.

We Wear Alchemy Jewellery, Choke Collars and
Necklaces,
A Fashionable Statement of Youth That Once Were.

I Live for The Night
And Sleep During Day,
I Don't Want to Turn Back Now,
As I'm Happy This Way.

Material Girl.

You lived in your Material world
You liked Fast Guys and Fast Cars
You worked Hard to keep up with Mrs Jones
You were too Busy for Friends and Family
your Beauty was only Skin Deep
You slept in that Luxurious bed
I won't say it yours cause it was
on Borrowed Money as your Bank was in the Red

You Pretended to the World you were doing so Well
but Slowly you were going Down Hill
you just couldn't stop at any Cost
going Spending Big in all those shops
the Fake Smile you wore with Pride
while you were Crying Inside
Nothing was ever going to be Enough
and in the end it was too Much
when you Died your Headstone said
26 yrs. old and Had it All
but Eventually she had Nothing at all
when you Died your Headstone said
this is the Full Price She Paid.

Winter's Snow.

Snowflakes are falling soft and slow
laying a white blanket down below.

Gently covering the rooftops,
oh, how lovely is the sight

As night frost shines so bright,
glistening leaves in their sight

Our breath showing as we talk,
lovers out for a nightly walk

As snowflakes
twinkle silently all around

softly crisping is the sound.

Angel.

My Angel comes to me every time I call

She listens to all the thoughts that are in my mind
as she gently soothes my heart and lifts my spirits high

My dearest Angel on whom I can depend
When I feel broken, she's the one who'll mend

No matter how low or lost I am
she'll always be there guiding me with her charm

She never gives up on me
her kindness and the beauty of the way she always shares
and this shows just how much she really cares

My angel's voiceless song with a message so divine
Singing I will take care of you until the end of time.

My Darkness.

I'm trembling to the bone
as I sit here alone
What was that I just saw?
A dark creepy silhouette in my hall

I'm frozen in my state
You glanced a glare upon me
Sent shivers down my spine
Then you grabbed hold
And drank the blood that's mine

I felt every drop fade away as did my soul.
Moments later as I woke
Was it all a dream?

Went about my day as usual thank-full to be here,
shopping, writing, visiting
Then when the moon came out that night,
I began to Howl.

So be careful if you go out tonight
Because I am on the prowl.

Christmas Time.

Children wait and anticipate as Christmas time approaches
Wondering what Santa will bring for them...

They watch as snowflakes fall gently outside
Capturing the scene they have so long dreamed...

Under the Christmas tree, presents they see
Christmas time is here....an exciting time of year.

Children playing in the snow with their faces all aglow.
Come inside now and have a hot drink to warm you from
the cold.
Mum and Dad have No problems getting their kids to bed
tonight.

Christmas Eve approaching, children pretending to
sleep...with thoughts of presents that excite and entice
them to stay awake.
Waiting on Santa dropping Presents of under the Tree.
Filling Stocking on their beds.... covers twitching...eyes a
peeking ...better watch out Santa's about!

Christmas mornings arrived...all the children cheer as they
race to the Tree
I wonder what Santa has left for me.

Different Strokes For Different Folks.

A painter may like to see some different seasons and
scenery,
A poet may like a few well-chosen words to help finish his
verse,
A writer may like to hear some interesting facts to help
with his chosen topic, even involving a little bit of gossip.

An artist, a poet, a writer, letting their imaginations run
free.
Thus, producing a picture, a book, a poem for everyone to
see.
A picture, a book, a poem all from imagination were
sewn.
The greatest architects of all time are the ones hidden in
the imaginations of our mind!

It's About Time.

Come Rain, Hail or Shine
It's All About Time!
The Seasons We Know
Will Come and Go
Whether We're Young
Or Growing Old.

Look at The Hands
On the Clock on The Wall
They Tick So Fast They So Quick
Time Does Play Its Timely Trick!
Time Can Go by So Fast or Slow.
It's What We Do with That Time
That Makes the Difference.

So Don't Let Opportunities Slip
Grab Them Fast Grab Them Quick!

Dancing With Wolves.

I've Had Dances with Wolves
Well At Least Two That I Can Remember!

They Knocked at My Door and Persuaded Me to Let Them
In
Of Course, They Were Neatly Disguised as Honest Men.

Then We Started to Dance and Sing and Got Along Great
And I Never Suspected a Thing

On the Computer We Chatted and That's Where It All
Started
Their Dishonesty of Men

I Trusted Their Words of Love and Caring Upon A Life We
Could Both Be Sharing
Then After a Year, it all Became Clear
I Realised Then I'd Been Taking in By Wolves Neatly
Disguised as Men!

Writers Block.

Writers Block
Oh, What A Shock!
As I Can't Think What to Say!
As I Try to Put My Thoughts on The Line
It's Like My Minds Gone Blind!
As I can't Find the Words Today!

Perception Ain't Perfection.

Do we perceive ourselves through other people's eyes?
Even though we take this on, did we ever think they might
be wrong?
I'm not like that! Please look again! And see me for who I
am!

The good, bad and ugly perceptions
Hold onto the positive ones that make us sure
Forget about all that negative allure
If we can accept this and just move on
Then any negative perceptions should be gone

I've lived my life in some unsafe ways
On the streets of life I forgot to look both ways

And as the sun so slowly came to rise
it shone the tear drops from my eyes

I' m going to look again and see me for who I am!
Because yes really, I do give a damn!

Elvis Aaron Presley.

Elvis the rock legend
I believe he was the best in his day
The King of Rock 'n' Roll
My favourite movie King Creole
His death left many memories of his talent
His life was never going to be silent
He worked hard to improve his life
He helped out his best friends and of course his wife
Who were all sad at his bitter end
As they'd lost a lover and very good friend
His fame and fortune were partly to blame for
The way he died
He will always be remembered as he inspired
Lots of people with his talents
He could sing and dance leaving people in a trance
Feeling the night was full of romance
He had a kind and true heart
And not one made of wood
He had a ground of pride on which he stood
American Trilogy is one of my favourite songs
For Elvis Aaron Presley I will remember his song
Return to sender.

Part II

Stories

Mermaid.

Joe set sail early that morning; he was sure this time he would be in luck, to catch some fish as the rain had hailed down all night! With waterproof pants, knee length wellies and worms for bait and of course his old trusted rods he set off.

Sure enough as luck would have it, Salmon were jumping high up over the Loch, at Loch Katrine. Joe got his rod and bait of worms ready; swoosh went rod into the water and moments later, Horary he shouted as the rod was being tugged, Horary again he shouted as he wound in his catch of a Salmon Trophy. I wonder how many more I can catch, as I could go home with a batch. So of he went again swoosh went his rod, and he waited and waited, and waited and waited, nothing more and nothing yet still.

I think I must have scared the other fish away, damn it, I think I'll sail further up and see if I have a stroke of better luck. So Joe set sail further up the Loch to see if his luck would be better of there.

A wee flask o' tea and my little sandwich of lettuce, cheese and tomatoes and Branston pickle will do for the now, while he sat staring into the Loch his eyes skimming the water to see if any fish were there. Then Suddenly, Swoosh! a Mermaid jumped up from the deep, she dove again then was gone.

Joe waited with bated breath, he waited for just a glimpse, but nothing happened. I must been daydreaming he said, and then just as he'd said that; Swoosh! again, the Mermaid was swimming as if caressing the sea, swimming swift yet silent. It seemed although she was dancing on the waves and trying to entice Joe to follow where she led. Joe thought, maybe she knows where the best place for me to catch fish is; maybe I should chase or follow after her. With that said Joe set sail, with winds of change and chance the Mermaid lead a merry dance. Eventually she came to rest and Joe decided this must be the spot so he stopped his boat. Another flask of tea and some biscuits this time, Joe drank his tea and decided to fish in this spot.

Hours later to his dismay, nothing caught. The Mermaid, though he thought fondly of her, oh why, oh why did she come to me. Then again he waited with bated breath just for another glimpse of her. Her beauty deep beyond comparison, her eyes sparkling, her hair golden silk and her fin does twinkling. Oh fair maiden of the sea I beg for one more glimpse of thee.

Joe just sat as if in despair as he waited and waited for her to appear. I've never seen anything quite like thee, he thought as he waited for her just another glimpse please of thee, but as he sat and waited and waited more nothing did he see, or another glimpse of thee.

Dog Tales – Star.

Hi, my name is Star, I am 8 yrs. old I'm a mixed breed dog. I'm Beige and White in colour and this is my story!

My owners a couple named Tom and Liz and their 6 yrs. old daughter Paige. I was adopted by them as a 6 month old pup from an advert the saw in the paper.

I loved it here, I was spoiled with tug rope toys, nice comfy dog bed, great food and dog chews, bones and biscuits, I really couldn't ask for more. Then when Paige came home from School, she'd take me to the park and we'd play ball. Also she had a large hula hoop she would hold up for me and I'd jump through it, and then she'd applaud me for doing so. She was my best friend in the whole wide world. We'd head home for dinner and I'd get my dinner and any leftovers from Paige's, yum.

At night Paige would do her homework and while she was doing so Liz would brush me and pet me and play my tug rope with me, Tom didn't usually finish work until later. When Paige had her bath she would let me in beside her as she'd throw some bubbles onto my head and laugh, it was great fun.

In the mornings when Tom and Liz went to work and Paige went to School I'd be left in their very large kitchen on my own. Just in case of any little accidents as I couldn't get out to the toilet.

Liz worked part-time in an office somewhere, and she'd come home four hours later, she'd feed me and let me out in the garden, and play tug rope with me, she was a good mum.

Anyway this day about five yrs. later, Liz had got a phone call and I could hear her saying, "That's great, the house is ready for us ok we'll get ready to move." I never thought anything about it really.

Anyway Paige came home from School, she'd be 11 yrs. by now, and Liz explained to her that the house was ready for them to move into, Paige said, "We are taking Star aren't we mum."

Liz looked at Paige and said, "Sorry honey, we can't, we're moving abroad to Australia. We can't take Star all that distance with us, he probably wouldn't survive the flight."

Well Paige burst into tears, and ran over and hugged me so hard she nearly hugged the life out of me, "What's going to happen to Star then mum," she asked?

I've arranged for the gentleman Bill next door to take him and that way Star doesn't have to get used to being in s different area. Paige said ok mum, but I could tell she wasn't too happy about the idea, come to think about it I wasn't sure I was either.

I had met Bill when I'd been in the garden, he'd come to his fence in his garden next door and chucked over the odd bone for me, he seemed ok, but I didn't want to lose my play mate of nearly five yrs. I didn't want to stay with Bill. No-one asked me what I wanted, I was just supposed to accept the idea, and it wasn't fair. Anyway I might survive the flight to Australia, if they can don't see why not. I really wasn't very happy about this idea at all.

Anyway Tom came home from work later that night around nine and Liz explained to him, Tom said, "Great

Liz. That's brilliant, our plans are coming together now and we will have that business of our own we've always dreamed about and a month from now we'll be there."

Paige went up to her dad complaining about leaving me with Bill, but her dad just said, listen Paige, we can't take Star all that distance with us, we're sorry hun.

Suddenly the family I thought had loved me so much never seemed to love me anymore, all except Paige, she's the only one who stuck by me, and Liz had stopped playing with me as much. In-fact a couple of weeks before they moved, Liz suggested it might be a good idea for me to go and live next door with Bill, to get me used to the idea before they moved.

So that was that, I was moved into Bill's with all my belongings, bed toys, and bedding. Paige would come and see me at Bills every day after School and still take me to the park and play ball and then return me to Bill after.

Paige asked Bill how I was, if I was eating alright. Bill said yes he's fine and I'm glad to have the little fella ain't I, Star? Of-course I couldn't talk, but at that time I thought Bill seemed ok, he fed me and talked to me.

Anyway the day came when Paige didn't come to take me out and I knew then that they had moved away, Bill also told me Paige has moved now Star, I'll be the one taking you out to the park. Bill took me to the park with my ball, we played a little while but it wasn't the same as being at the park with Paige, I missed her so much.

At night Bill would sit and watch the television and drink a little whisky, blether a lot of nonsense, and then go to bed, there was no night-time kiss on the head from him.

Anyway two yrs. had passed and I was about seven by now. Bill's drinking had got worse and he'd forgot to feed me and sometimes he didn't waken up till later on in the day by which time I was desperate to get out.

One day Bill had been drinking and got himself into a frenzy about something or another and he kicked me. For what I don't know. I had done a little widdle on the carpet, maybe that's why but he hadn't let me out what was I supposed to do? Anyway a few days later Bill let me out and I decided to run away, I'd had enough.

I became what you would call a stray. I lived on the streets. I'd find food thrown away by people who had been for a night out; scraps, chips, kababs, odd sandwiches, anything at all. I lived like that for a few months and was tiring from it, I was nearly eight yrs. old, I'd be lucky if I lived until I was nine. The winter was coming and I was getting desperate for warmth, warm and dry shelter, clean water and some company.

I'd been watching this elderly lady going into her garden to water her flowers. She looked like she was on her own and could also do with some company. So one day I decided to go to her front door and sit and yelp. She opened the door saying, "Oh, what's wrong with you then? You had better come in." I limped in pretending I had a sore paw. The lady who must have been about 60 yrs. as she had deep wrinkles and a full head of white curly hair. Anyway this lovely elderly lady let me into her house, gave me some clean water to drink and a little mince she had left over from the night before. "My name is Masie," she said, "what's your name?" She tried to guess, but of-course she had no idea. She knew by the state I was in that I had been sleeping rough.

It was great. Maisie showered me, brushed me and petted me. She even let me sleep on her bed and cuddled me. Maisie bought a soft ball for me to play with in the house with her, and she named me Bailey. I quite liked my new name and having a name again meant that I had someone to take care of me, and that was brilliant.

Realm Of Shadows.

Introduction: Hi my name is Blake Franklin Fox and this is my story. Purely fictional of course as I am a Mythical Creature, I am A Vampire.

I was born in the 19th Century in the year 1850 in the Victorian Town of "Spillingbrook" in Devon. My dad worked as a carpenter, he made all kinds of furniture from dressers to tables and chairs and on the odd occasion when asked would help with carving of wood for new buildings or children's toys. My mother was a seamstress; she worked mainly from home, sewing garments such as; baby rompers and gowns, ladies' bloomers, corsets and undergarments, bonnets, veils and shawls.

We lived in a lovely Victorian Cottage here in Spillingbrook, our cottage has a beautiful garden, which both my mother and my father took great pride in, my father had a small workshop at the bottom of the garden and an area for growing our own veg. We owned one horse with small cart and two hens, or I think a cock and a hen on the hope they would reproduce. I attended Spillington School, my interest were in reading poetry, and then after school my dad would draw up in horse and cart, then I would go to help my dad with Woodwork until it was time for dinner. Mother Had cooked our dinner on one of those Oberlin stoves, which worked on wood or coal.

I left school in 1864 at the age of 14 yrs. to work with my dad full-time as a carpenter and in my spare time I enjoyed reading and started to write poetry. I worked with my dad until his death in 1873, he died of flu due to his low immune system through having bone cancer in the April of that year, and my mother died the same year in August she had ovarian cancer. All of my known relatives were now deceased, and I decided I didn't want to follow in my father's footsteps and be a carpenter Besides the idea was too painful for because of the so many memories of my father, and not that I would ever forget him, just it was easier at this point in time to run away from accepting what had happened than accept facing the reality that my father was indeed dead.

At this point I just wanted out from the bungalow as much as possible and applied for a position as a barman at a nearby dancehall and bar called "The Lucky Brook". I started my position there and had come to quite enjoy it, I'd grown quite found of the beverages and being chatted up by the single ladies. We'd have a bit good old-fashioned banter, and the lucky few I'd take home and read some of my poetry to them. I suppose I was letting my hair down, become a bit of a "Jack-the-lad" and a possible alcoholic, I didn't care, I was enjoying myself!

However this day the year now 1975, I'd just finished my shift in the 'Lucky Brook' and was making my way home, when I heard a shot, then all of a sudden everything went bleary and quiet, then the next thing I knew, I was being dragged behind this tree and this voice was saying to me, "You've been shot lad but you're going to be ok, I'm gonna save you." That's the day that my life ended and my eternity/immortality began!

The rain was hammering down in the streets and splashed down on the dirty images of the buildings. I talked to myself as I walked the familiar streets of Devon with my eyes closed. Obscenities filled the chilled air around me, I enjoyed the rain, although I cursed the pollution of the streets. I was still aware of their infection through my closed lids and hated that there was flashing lights where there should have been darkness.

As I stepped over the threshold of this club I used to know I sighed heavily... I was still working there though as The Proprietor now, as the last Owner left "The Lucky Brook" to me in his Will, I had Originally worked as a barman and have been since 1874, the year after my mother and father had died both from Cancer, so much had changed over these years and the club has had a few owners of all whom I have known.

Another night ahead watching all these idiots prancing around in their Gothic clothes of Red Purple and Black Lace, their painted White faces running down in the sweat of the lights and bodies. They smell like a meal to me, like animals. Even the clean ones smell like a sweaty meal to me. I can't stand it/them.

Although the lights were soft and dim I squinted as they hurt my eyes and glowered over my shoulder towards the innocent light switch. I walked over to the bar and tossed my keys down onto the counter.

"I knew I would find you eventually."

I spun around in the direction of the voice. It wasn't just hearing his voice that startled me but the fact that I had not immediately sensed the presence of another being in the club with me. I'd been around my clientele and nobody else for too long. They've dulled my senses, made me soft, and made me like them. I was no longer the predator I used to be. Living with them, being near them had made me only a fraction of my former self.

That voice was unmistakable. By the time I'd turned around and the realization had hit me fully my blood had frozen in my veins, rom the soles of my feet up to the tip of my head. I was unsure whether the sensation was heat or cold. I swallowed hard and tried my damnedest to put forward an air of coolness, calmness, and nonchalance. I tried but I knew I would not fool the man who now stood before me, a man I had not seen for decades yet knew I would see again…someday.

Over the years I had almost learned the art of forgetting the fear that the mere mention of his name instilled in me and anybody else who knew of him. But those years withered and died, dissolved in a heartbeat, and left behind them an overwhelming nausea in the pit of my gut.

“Why did you come back? What do you want? I don't want you here.”

"Questions, questions, Blake. I've not even taken my coat off yet. And you've not offered me one of your fine beverages."

Although I hadn't uttered a word, the other man had read my thoughts. I hated it when he did that. I could feel my body quivering as I stood looking at him, instantly under his spell once again.

“Lucas. I thought…”

“Thought what, Blake? That I was dead? No, I'm not dead, well, I am, but you know what I mean,” Lucas told me with a broad smile bereft of any warmth or levity.

I was paler than usual and tiny beads of sweat sparkled on my brow and upper lip in the dim and dusty light inside the club. My uneasy aura pleased him immensely. He was happy that he could illicit such a strong reaction from his old friend after all this time.

"I won't be alone very long, so if you're going to kill me, just do it before somebody comes in to clean up the mess. We're opening soon."

Lucas's laughter broke through the silence. He slapped the bar with his open palm to punctuate his hysterics.

"Oh, Blake; you still make my belly ache with laughter," He said, rubbing at his stomach. He stopped laughing abruptly.

"If I wanted you dead, Blake, you wouldn't be standing there almost pissing yourself with fear," Lucas told me. He stared at me with those soulless eyes. I had no doubt that he meant what he said and I knew that I still stood there in my own club only by Vivant's grace. But what bothered me more than the thought of being killed by Lucas was why he was here in the first place. What bothered me the most was what Lucas wanted.

We stood looking at each other across the edge of the bar for what seemed like eternity. I still didn't know what he wanted and was still afraid to ask.

"You'll be wondering what the hell I'm doing here, yes?" he asked me.

"Of course, I'm wondering what you're doing here. We've not seen each other for decades. What is it you want?

"I want you, Blake. I want you back."

I stiffened at his words, my hands at my sides contracting into fists, shoulders drawing up as all my muscles all became taut, tense.

"I'm not sure what you mean." I tried my hardest not to stumble over his words, not to show my fear!

His rigidness made me vomit. Although there was no pulse that coursed through him, I felt that his veins were about to burst and that I had with my devout worship brought him back into the land of the living from the realm of the dead.

Had he been alive though, had he been *alive*, I would not have been so desperate to be part of his presence. Had he been alive, he wouldn't have scared me, enticed me or turned me into the deathly sight of a man that I remain today.

I wanted to be in his deathly embrace, I wanted to feel alive, I wanted to hear him gasp my name in the dark, I wanted him to need me the way I needed him. I shivered at his rigid torso like that of a cold marble statue. My mouth fell open in surprise and in shock at the glacial cold that seeped into my loins. It spread through me, invaded me, infected me like a virus for which there is no cure. It exhilarated and pacified me like an addict's fix.

I was dizzy, completely absorbed a vision, no more than a lowly angel - an archangel. I was frenzied, maddened at the thought of going so long without feeding and fighting with myself, at the idea of defiling an innocent human for the sake of my appetite. I was very weak. If I did not try this, I felt that I would die.

We stood glaring at each other. I was determined not to give Lucas the fight he wanted, and Lucas was desperate for each of us to draw blood and tear strips of each other in a deranged crazed, obsessive battle of wits and fists. Then Lucas started taunting me.

"Oh Blake, you're so weak, and how many deaths have happened right outside this club of yours in these past decades and you couldn't get up the courage to drink or feed from anyone of them? Oh and Blake, I have a gift for you".

Just then Lucas brought in this young Lady of around 22yrs of age, he explained she'd been stabbed by this knife thug and he'd been there to save her dying, just as he had been with me.

Lucas then said, "Show some appreciation Blake. Go on feed from her, she's my gift to you to help rebuild your strength and don't kill her, turn/save her then she can be your immortal companion."

I shuddered and convulsed all that had happened came back to me like the melancholy whisper of a ghost. The tears served to dilute my pain, carrying it away in a deluge of bitter grief and my flowing was the purge of my sins, the cleansing of my soul.

And I knew the one I would always remember that he was the one that I saved me and that I would always remain among the immortal/undead.

"Blake don't be so coy - it's unbecoming on you."

I tried hard to swallow but my mouth was dry, nervous tension was obstructing my throat. The nerves in my lower abdomen stirred as Lucas's words triggered his memories. And he remembered in glorious hues of red. As he thought back to those times, he could not stop himself from sighing. A low growl made its way up his throat as his primal nature began returning, triggered by remembering me and Lucas on their legendary hunts. I remembered both of us lying on our backs, chests heaving with exertion, soaked from head to foot with fresh blood and picking shreds of flesh and clumps of hair from between our teeth. I remembered having a human heart in my hands, staring at it with fascination and squeezing the last of the contents of the organ into my mouth. And I remembered the two of us, fangs locked into each other's veins and feverishly drinking in the potent vampire blood. No sensation on earth - human or vampire - could compare to that of one vampire feeding from another. The sensation was beyond bliss, quite simply, beyond comparison.

A knowing grin spread across Lucas's ruddy face.

"You don't have to lament the passing of those days anymore Blake. I'm back. We're together again. And we can feel what we once felt."

Tears welled up in my eyes as I realized I was again powerless to resist him. My mind and body screamed at me to be strong, but the vampire heart that beat inside me told me to go out into the night and be what I was supposed to be - a ruthless killer, a murderer, a beast. The feral heart that beat out a tattoo inside my chest told me to go out into the night and be the only thing that he could be - a vampire.

I walked, stepping heavily across the floor, and slumped down on a low stool at a table in a corner of the club. I had no idea what I was going to do. A war was raging inside my head between the man I was now and the beast I knew I could be. I knew which one was stronger. I knew which one would be triumphant. Questions filled my mind and my brow furrowed as a satisfactory answer evaded me.

What is it that stops me from being what I am and doing what I know I want to do?

These humans do nothing but make me insane with their smell and their falseness and their pretence and their...their...very being! I'd love to run rampant through this club when it's full to capacity and slit each and every throat from ear to ear and bathe in the arterial spurts that would paint the walls a beautiful shade of vampire red.

"So, come with me then, Blake. Don't just dream about the old days - let's live them again. Let's be more than we were even then. We're older now, stronger, and more powerful. The world is ours and there is nothing beyond our grasp. It is all there for the taking and if you want it, all you have to do is reach out and take hold of it. Come with me."

Lucas held out his hand to me, crooking his fingers toward himself in a come-hither gesture. I didn't move. I couldn't move. I sat there, body rigid, hands on his knees and my fingernails digging into the flesh on my legs. I still tried to resist him, I still tried to deny Lucas his domination over me, but I knew it was futile.

As I rose, shoulders slumped, my head heavy, defeated by myself and my own desires. Lucas knew only too well what I was going through, the torture, the torment.

I watched as the near-black of Lucas's irises bled into the whites turning them dark and the iris flooded with scarlet colour. His pupils became feline, elongated and a snarl curled his upper lip as he showed me a stab of keen white enamel.

Before I could blink, I was slammed into the club wall with such a brute force that each one of my ribs shattered and I felt sharp shards of bone protruding through his skin and the heat of my own blood running down my front. Immediately my immortal bones began to knit back together again and within seconds I was new again, unharmed.

"You think it's going to be that easy, you fucking prick?" Lucas's voice emerged from a growl that rumbled in his throat.

"But...but...I thought..."

"You thought you'd just swan back in and everything would be rosy in the garden and we'd go on our merry way our way through eternity, right? Wrong! You've got some fucking explaining to do. And if I'm not satisfied with your answers, then...well, let's just say your answers had better be satisfactory, you understand me?"

I knew that he was serious.

"I'll ask you again - do you understand me?" He asked again.

"Yes, I understand. I'm sorry, Lucas."

"Sorry? What for? Trying to kill me?"

"Yes, I'm sorry for that. I had no right to do it. I just wanted to get away from you."

"You could have just left me a fucking note! But no, you had to try and kill me. Why did you do that? Were you that afraid of me? What did I ever do to you to make you hate me so much?"

I felt ashamed of myself and looked down, toed the pool of my own congealing blood that lay on the floor at my feet.

"I'm sorry. I don't know what else to say. But you do know what you did, Lucas. I saved your sorry ass Blake, but maybe you wish I hadn't! I know I don't deserve your mercy, so if you're gonna kill me for what I did, so be it. I won't struggle. I accept my fate."

Lucas looked at me with a horrified look.

"What? Jesus, you've been amongst mortals way too long".

"I'm glad it's finally over. I've lived with the fear of you coming back for so fucking long that I nearly forgot what I was afraid of," I said as I laughed bitterly. "I just want it finished. So finish it now, Lucas. Kill me."

"You'd like that, wouldn't you? Ever the fucking martyr. Well, fuck you; if that's what you want, I'm not going to give it to you."

But as we stood there, minds reading each other, we both knew that it was futile. A bond that can never be broken was between us - the bond of father and son, the bond of brotherhood, of lovers, of family - the bond of the maker and the child. These were bonds that had withstood ultimate betrayal, loss, loneliness and the expanse of decades. But in the moments as they looked at each other, the years disappeared into history and this night - the night they were brought together again - was just the beginning.

A Thrilling Time.

"Argh!!!!" I screamed as I got pushed against the cold wet wall. I looked down to my stomach, to find my hand covered in blood, what had I done? And then I realized, it wasn't anything I had done...it's what someone else had done. I had been attacked. My black top now had an increasing blood stain on it. I looked up and saw somebody running away. I couldn't quite make out who it was since it was so dark. As I looked to see the perpetrator a raindrop landed on my nose. One by one, the raindrops became faster and colder. I looked around and realized that I was in an alleyway. All of a sudden, the pain began to have more of an effect and my vision ended up going bleary. I slowly slid down the wall, the floor vanishing beneath me. As I fell, I saw something in the distance and it was coming towards me.

At this point I didn't know whether to be relieved or scared. As the figure came up to me I felt something soft on my cheek. It was his shirt. As I looked around I could see that it was just the two of us. From what I could make out he had dark brown hair and brown eyes. He lifted me up and found my wound. Hoping it wouldn't be too late he took me to his place of residence. When he held me close to his chest, slowly but gently rocking me backwards and forwards he said, "Don't worry, it's going to be ok,"

I was sure I'd heard that voice before but where from? I thought about it for a while and then I realized it was Johnny. His voice was so peaceful and calm it made me forget about the rain falling, even the reason why I was there. Within a few minutes I lost consciousness but by then I was past caring. I knew I was safe. If I had died or if I survived then hopefully I'd be able to remember what had happened and give the police some help on solving this crime. When I woke, I felt tainted, flawed and impure. And then I felt repulsed and started to vomit. With a trembling voice I asked Johnny what was happened to me. Johnny's reply came slow, "You've been violated by a Werewolf."

I fainted at these words, darkness loomed, I awoke again in crippling pain, crawling along the floor as I had become nothing less than a Werewolf myself. As the darkness crept towards me my last breath surges in. I see my life flash before me and all I see is another Werewolf before me.

While Thunder crashes overhead I ask, "Is that you? Are you Johnny"?

"Yes it's me. I'm Johnny," he replies.

"Did you violate me I asked?"

"Yes," he replied. "I'm so sorry Katie."

"You fucking bastard. Why? Why?"

"I didn't mean it Katie, honest, I couldn't help it. I needed you. It's been so long since I've fed. Thankfully I didn't kill you!"

"It might have been better if you had, you bastard! Now I've got to live like an animal. Just like you."

"Katie please, you don't understand. You are one of the few survivors; mostly everyone else on earth has either been killed by our kind or violated and are now living in the darkness and unleashing their monster within. We have to stick together, Katie, we must as there are a few bounty hunters looking for *our kind.* They are trying to get rid of us to have humans inhabit the earth once again."

"Johnny, why are you giving into accepting that there's nothing we can do about our state?"

"Katie, there isn't anything, we just have to fucking accept that!"

"Well I'm not staying here in this fucking makeshift home cave with you. I'm leaving! I can't live like an animal and I won't accept that this is going to be my life from now on. Johnny, who attacked you?"

"I have no fucking idea! I was just coming home from the night club down this fucking lane and it all happened so fast I never saw the fucking assailant."

"How long ago did this happen to you?"

"About a year ago, Katie. It was around 1am on the 1st March, 2000."

"Ok and how do you know there are others?"

"Well, when I'd been out at night looking for a feed I'd witnessed others attacking humans. Also on a full moon my inner instincts have drawn me to this area where Werewolves run and meet in packs howling under the full moon before they go on the hunt for humans. There is usually an Alpha Male Leading the pack and there are usually around 10 packs. I've seen and around 20 Wolves in each pack. It fucking terrifies me; I usually hide in the bushes!"

"Did they see you and did you speak to them?"

"No, I hid. I was scared to approach them."

"And these bounty hunters, how do you know about them?"

"I saw some around and they were saying they have new technology for tracking down Werewolves. They have loaded guns with silver bullets and silver stakes. They're gonna go out at night when the moon is full. These bounty hunters will go out in groups to seek and kill all the Werewolves off!"

"Ok, Johnny, so do you know when there is going to be a full moon?"

"Katie, there are around 12 or more fucking full moons a year. I have a calendar showing all the dates. The next one due is Thursday, Feb 8th 2001 and that's only 2 weeks away. And then the next one is Friday, the 9th of March."

"Ok and what else do you eat apart from humans? In fact, have you ever eaten a human?"

"No Katie, I've never eaten a human. If truth be told you're the first human I've ever violated. I've been surviving on attacking deer and devouring them, but my inner instincts aren't accepting this anymore, I can smell a human within a 20 mile radius and they smell so good. The aroma smells oh so good."

"Ok Johnny, I'm leaving now but I will return,"

"When Katie?"

"As soon as I can."

"Please be careful out there, Katie and try not to morph into a Werewolf while you're gone or you'll blow our cover and the hunters will track us down."

"It's ok Johnny, it's nearly dark now and I'll return before morning. I just need to get home showered and check the internet for information on Werewolves. I'll be back by morning. If you're lucky I'll bring some raw steak with me."

"Ok Katie, just be bloody careful."

"I'm back told you I would be!"

"Yeah I knew you were coming, my instincts told me. I've been pacing the fucking floor all night worrying that you'd morph and get caught. Thank fuck you're ok!"

"Well, I got the information that I went home to find. And I brought a present for you."

"Yeah I can smell the steak. Thank you, Katie."

"Here then."

"That was fucking delicious."

"Yeah, it only took you two seconds to devour it. Where are your table manners?"

"Anyway Katie where's that information you found?"

"It's here. I searched several sites for this. It states here that Lycanthropy is a man morphing, shape-shifting or transforming from man to animal and that Werewolves are humans who have either been bitten or scratched by a Werewolf or that one of either male or female parent being one. Occult findings state that: A wicked person worshiping the Devil and surrendering their soul may be granted the immortal power of being able to morph from human to Werewolf. I never got any real evidence on how or why Werewolves evolved, but shit if it's from Devil worship."

"Anyway there's more info here; it says that magic salve or ointment is used by Werewolves by being rubbed on their bodies before transformation helping stop the pain of transforming. The ointment used is a plant extract called nightshade. The final piece of information I've found on this is important. It states that Werewolves can be killed by driving a stake through their heart and ripping it out so it can't recover, and also that Werewolves can or may be changed back to human form if a piece of iron or steel is thrown over them from back to front."

"Great, so we may actually be able to control our transformation. That's brilliant, Katie."

"Yeah, I thought so. Only it would take two packs of wolves for this to be successful as you couldn't throw steel or iron over yourself. So it looks like I'm stuck with you. That however doesn't make you the Alpha Male and anyhow you're too much of a chicken for that!' "Yeah thanks for that vote of confidence Katie, I accept that you're right though I am a coward. I was scared that once you went back to the comfort of your home you wouldn't return!"

"Yeah I was tempted to stay there. I'm worried about my mum. She's bound to notice I'm not around. She left me a message on my answer machine. I called her from my mobile saying I was on holiday and apologized that I forgot to call her before I went. I told her I'd be back in a few days and that my holiday was work related. Then I phoned my work and left a message saying I've got the flu and hope to be back next week. Johnny, this is shit for me. I have a life. I'm just thankful I wasn't married with kids when you attacked me, you fucking idiot."

After my shower I looked in the mirror. I freaked out. My arms legs feet and back of my hands are covered in hair though thankfully my face appeared normal. Well, apart from looking a bit longer and my breath stank. I'm so fucking angry!

"I'm sorry Katie, honestly if I could take back what I've done."

"Yeah, well you can't."

"Katie, I'm going out to chop some more wood for the fire. I won't be long. You can come if you want."

"Yeah, maybe for the best. Anyway, I don't want to sit here on my own."

"Ok, great. Here, we'll need this wheelbarrow."

"Johnny, have you ever been home since this happened to you?"

"Yeah Katie, when it first happened. I went home and tried to act normal by going to work and visiting family and friends only I started acting weird and became very angry for no apparent reason and ended up attacking and nearly killing this guy at work, and just because he was late after our break. I worked as a car mechanic and a car had to be ready for collection that afternoon. Needless to say I got the sack. Then I had a run in with my dad because he called me an idiot for losing my job. I couldn't believe how angry I felt towards him. Thankfully I left before I hit him. I phoned and told them I've got a new girlfriend in Paris and that I'm over there staying with her just now and trying to find work. Like you though I also noticed more hair on my body and thanks to the newsagent mentioning it - I know my breath stinks. Then as I had no money to pay my rent I decided to move up here."

"Isn't there a chance that other Werewolves will know we're here?"

"Yeah, there's a chance, but we just have to hope they won't detect us. I think this is enough firewood for now, we probably need some more in a few days."

"Argh!! What's that?"

"What's what, Katie?"

"That noise. Don't you hear it? It's like someone's following us."

"Shh, Katie. Yeah I hear it. It's probably nothing to worry about. It's probably some bird or something."

"SOME BIRD EH?" came this erupting laugh from the bushes.

"Well, well, well, what do we have here? A couple of Were-humans eh? What are your names? Mmm let me think - Dog and his Bitch?"

"Shut up. And in any case who are you?"

"Dare You Ask? I'm Valdini the Saxon Alpha Male of my pack although I'm appearing to you in my human form."

"Where's your pack Leader? Has he sent you couple of love birds out on your own?"

"Well, no. We're here of our own accord."

"Really? So do you want to join my pack?"

"No thanks, we're fine on our own, aren't we Katie?"

"Yeah, thanks Valdini, but we're ok."

"In that case why can I smell fear from you both? I can read your thoughts, I take it you didn't know that? Let me see what did I read from you both? Oh yeah, it was "'Let's get the fuck out of here,'" wasn't it? What's wrong you aren't scared of me are you? Mind you if I were you I'd probably be scared too."

"Sorry Valdini, we've been up here so long on our own we like it that way that's all."

"Ok then, but if you change your minds. I don't bite honest. In fact you could say my growl is worse than my bite. Anyway, if you do want to team up then my pack is over there for around two miles to te left."

"Ok, Valdini thanks. We'll keep that in mind."

"Katie, are you ok?"

"Yeah, I'm fine as long as we get back double quick speed."

"Here we are and thank fuck for that. That was quite an ordeal. I didn't know what Valdini was gonna say or do."

"Yeah, you and me both. I don't want to stay up here a minute longer. What if other packs find out we're here, what then? And what if Valdini comes back? He scares the fucking shit out of me."

"Yeah, me too. So you are staying tonight aren't you Katie?"

"Yeah, just for tonight though. I'm leaving here as soon as possible. Besides, my mum will be expecting to see me soon, and I need to get rid of my extra body hair before then. I'll need to try some hair removal creams."

"Yeah, and if it works let me know."

"Yeah, ok you big sissy. I always knew you were a sissy."

"Oi you, that's enough. Anyway, when you go you probably won't be back, and truth is now I've got used to the company and probably won't want to live up here on my own anymore, and certainly now that that Valdini character knows where we are. Could you imagine me if another pack found me here on my own?"

"Yeah, you'd shit yourself and have a heart attack."

"Dunno about asking you this, Katie, but would it be alright if I came and stayed at yours?"

"Erm, I'm not sure. What if my mum sees you?"

"I'd go out if I knew she were gonna visit you. Oh Katie please. I promise to be on my best behaviour at all times."

"I don't believe I'm saying this but ok then. Best behaviour at all times though or you're out."

"Thanks Katie, I promise."

"Ok, just three hours till morning, we'll be needing a sleep when we get back to mine. Being nocturnal has its down sides, and I'm already worrying about how that's gonna effect my job. I might have to look for a new night-shift one and you'll have to try and find work too. You're not sitting in my apartment all day."

"Yes Mum, I promise to find a night shift job also."

"Good, that's that settled then."

"What the fuck is this? Why have you locked me up in this fucking cage, Johnny? And how?"

"Well, you were letting your imagination run riot about going home and living a normal life. I hate to tell you this Katie, but we're not normal humans anymore. We're Werewolves and we can change into one at any time of the day or night. How would your mum feel or react if she saw you morph into a Werewolf in front of her? She'd probably die of fright."

"Let me outta here, Johnny. I'm getting so fucking angry with you and my whole body's in pain. I'm in agony. What's happening to me?"

"You're morphing into a Werewolf. Stop shaking that cage. I'm not letting you out. I'm going out to find us some food, I'll be back soon."

"Johnny, you bastard, don't leave me locked up in here and on my own."

"Hey Katie, you've fully morphed now and you sound rough and terrifying. I'll let you out when you morph back. I promise. Now I'm off to catch prey."

"I could kill you, you fucking bastard."

"Yeah just as well I locked you in that cage then. Ok I'm off."

"Right here we are, some deer heart and steak, Katie. Calm down, you're gonna get some. Here, have a heart and a steak. Looks like you enjoyed that. It only took you 4 seconds to devour it. I've told you, Katie, the inner Werewolf instincts can't be denied or controlled. We have to accept that. And it's only a week and a half now until the next Full Moon. This is 27th Jan 2001 and the next Full Moon is Thurs the 8th Feb 2001. Aww, you're sleeping now, thank fuck, I think I'll take a nap too."

"Well are you gonna let me out this fucking cage NOW?"

"What's that? Oh, Katie you're awake, you nearly gave me a heart attack."

"Serves you right for locking me up in this fucking jail."

"Sorry Katie, but believe me when I say it was for your own good."

"Good? Just get me the fuck out."

"Ok, Katie seeing as you've morphed back."

"Don't you ever lock me up in that fucking contraption again; do you hear me, Johnny?"

"Yeah, Katie ok, calm down now."

"I've been listening to what you said Johnny about changing into a Werewolf at any time day or night. I've also been thinking that you're right I can't go and see my mum in case I morph in front of her. I'm so fucking angry with you Johnny, you've ruined my life and you've cursed my life by making me into a Werewolf. I need to go for a walk. I need some fresh air."

"Katie, let me come with you."

"No. I need to be on my own, I need to think."

"I understand, Katie, just be careful."

"Hey let go of me. Who do you think you are? Stop it. Where are you taking me?"

"Shh girl it's gonna be ok. We're just taking you on a little journey. We're giving you a sedative injection to make you sleep now. Just close your eyes."

"Damn it, I'm gonna look for her, that's nearly two hours Katie's been gone."

When I waken up I find myself locked in a barn...The door creaks open slowly and in walks Valdini.

"What the Hell do you think you're doing kidnapping me?"

"Well, it's nearly time for the next full moon and when the full moon arrives it's the best time for you to conceive my LUDAS child."

"Don't Valdini; you clearly don't know what you're asking. I'm from a Werewolf bloodline."

"Who and where?"

"My German grandfather, Valdromere. He is a very powerful Werewolf and his father before him. In fact you could almost say he is the Devil himself."

"Ok Katie, I'm sorry. Best not mention this oversight of mine to anyone, especially not your grandfather."

"I'll think about it, Valdini. If you do me any wrong my grandfather will sense it and come crashing down on you."

"Ok Katie, I've said I'm remorseful, just go."

"Hi Johnny, decided to go for a walk as well?"

"Well actually, I got worried about you and came looking. You look awful Katie, are you alright?"

"Well not really. That Creep Valdini abducted me."

"He did what?"

"He injected a sedative to make me sleep and then took me to this barn over there where he and his pack reside. Just as I woke up he came in and demanded I was going to conceive his LUDAS child on the next full moon."

"Fuck Katie, so did he let you go to come back for you?"

"No, I tricked him into letting me go."

"How?"

"I told him I have a strong Werewolf bloodline leading back to my great grandfather in Germany and that my grandfather would take vengeance on him if he harmed me in any way."

"So he believed you and released you? That's fucking brilliant, Katie. Thank fuck you're alright though."

"Yeah, damn right, Johnny. Let's just get back now."

With a Flash of Lightening and storm darkened skies, in the Dusseldorf Village in Germany, Adalrick Schafer, a German Scientist who's Girlfriend was taken three years ago by Werewolves, is making his way to work in the City of Nuremberg.

"Hallo Kollgen-(hello Colleagues)."

"Trauriges Adalrick, werden sie von hier uben wegen Ihrs verrruckten Fetisches fur Werewolves entlassen.-(sorry

Adalrick, you are being dismissed from practicing here because of your crazy fetish for Werewolves."

"Auf Wiedersehen Kollgen-(Goodbye colleagues)."

"I knew it was going to be a bad day for me when it was Thunder and Lightning on my way to work. Those pigs have had it in for me ever since my dear Fruendin-(Girlfriend) Adelheid Bauer was taken by Werewolves three years ago, oh my beloved Adelheid. I've been practicing medicine and trying to come up with a cure for Werewolves and my colleagues think I'm crazy, two fingers to them. So what do I do now!? No job. No money."

"Bagel, madam please, expresso and today's paper, thank-you."

"Aha, says here that they are looking for a person to work in the Missing Persons Investigation Bureau UK in their French Office Located in Mayenne."

"Here greedy gull, have some of my Bagel, I'm off to Mayenne."

"Katie! Katie! Wake the hell up."

"Ok, I think I'm up now, what is the urgency?"

"I've been to my newsagents and bought this paper...and well... I hate to tell you this but your mum has reported you as a missing person."

"Get to fuck. Let me see that. Blimey Johnny, according to this, my mother expected to hear from me around a week ago and is concerned that she hasn't apparently. She's been talking with my next door neighbour Mrs Jeanne Le Gall who mentioned the last time she saw me was the 25th of Jan, she must have seen me that night I went home to check the comp, bugger I told my mum I was on a working holiday then. No wonder she suspects something is wrong, today is Mon The 5th of Feb, it's just over a week since I contacted her and I'm getting worried myself as the next full moon is fast approaching."

"I'm a bit concerned about the next Full Moon also Katie, this will be your first and let me tell you, all the powers of Werewolf instincts will be pulling on you to be at that full moon along with all those other packs, and who knows how many? It's the not knowing what's gonna happen until that day comes that's the frightening thought."

"Hello, hello madam, I'd like to rent the flat you have advertised."

"Ah yes can you come and see me this evening at 5pm."

"Yes, madam Mortou that would be excellent. See you at 5pm."

"Bonjour monsieur Adalrick (Hello Mr Adalrick)! Parlez-vous Francais? (Do you speak French?) Pas vraiment Madame. (Not really madam) L'Allemand ou l'anglais est mon meilleur. (German or English is my best)."

"That's fine; we will stick by with English as my German is a bit rusty. So monsieur Adalrick, where do you work?"

"No sorry madam, at present I'm without employment, though I do have plenty of savings and I'm going for an interview tomorrow with The Missing Persons Investigation Bureau here in Mayenne."

"Alright monsieur, I'm going to give you the flat, but I'll expect two months' rent in advance and if that's ok with you then we have an agreement. I will copy the agreement out for you to sign and a copy for you to keep."

"Perfect and thank-you madam Mortou. I appreciate your offer, I promise to be a most excellent tenant."

"Hello monsieur, "Good morning monsieur Adalrick, please come with me, close the door behind you. Please sit; now what experience do you have that you can relate to this offer of employment?"

"I have worked as a scientist and research assistant in Nuremberg and I have gained experience in research and believe this will be of use if I'm employed by you. I have my C.V with me."

"Excellent monsieur Adalrick, yes I can see from your C.V that you have worked many years as a research scientist and have an interest in helping others and are reliable. Let me tell you about your possible position here: we work closely with partners and communities we provide support and advise to police forces. We act as the centre for the exchange of information connected with the search for missing persons nationally and internationally. The unit focuses on cross matching missing persons with unidentified persons/bodies. Other key activities include: you will be maintaining records of missing persons and unidentified persons/bodies to provide an investigative support service to police. You would be maintaining a dental index of ante-mortem chartings of long term missing persons and post-mortem chartings from unidentified bodies. You will partake in all training: we advise on opportunities to improve identification capabilities for biometric technology."

"That sounds great. I would be more than willing to partake in any training available and would give one hundred percent to my position here."

"Excellent monsieur Adalrick, I will be in contact."

"Thank-you for considering me for the position Mr Jarry and I look forward to hearing from you."

"This position would be excellent, fingers crossed, should know by tomorrow. Now I think I'll do some sightseeing and The Jardine botanique de la Perrine' is just down here and over to the left, ah there it is, what a beautiful sight to behold, a botanical garden and park. Think I'll sit here with my Cappuccino and try to clear my thoughts and get ready for a brand new tomorrow. I'm so excited and here is to new beginnings.

Ring, ring..."Hello, Bonjour can I speak to Mr Adalrick please?"

"Yes Monsieur this is he."

"This is Mr Jarry from the Missing Persons Investigation Bureau and I'm delighted to offer you the position with us"."

"That's great thank you so much Monsieur, when would you like me to start?"

"If you would like to start on Monday. Come along for 8am that would be great."
"Yes that's fine, Mr Jarry, that's fine."

"Ok, we will see you then."

"Hey Katie wake up. You've been having nightmares and I've hardly slept a wink."

"Sorry Johnny, I can't help worrying about this next full moon. I hope it is just nightmares and not visions I've been dreaming about."

"What do you mean, Katie? I think you had best let me know what you've been dreaming about."

"Oh Johnny, I'm so scared, I've been seeing people dying and Valdini and his pack are to blame."

"It's ok Katie, keep cuddling into me. I'm sure it's just been a bad dream."

"Oh Johnny, I hope you're right."

Bio –

I live in a small village in Scotland. My main interests are Art, Music, Nature and Poetry. One of the first books I read was "A Child's Garden of Verses," by author Robert Louis Stevenson. This really sparked my imagination as a young child. I love spending time with my family and close friends. I enjoy nature walks and watching nature/wildlife programmes narrated by Sir David Attenborough. I also enjoy going to live music venues when I can. I have a condition called Spasmodic Torticollis (Cervical Dystonia) which I developed at the age of 27 after a fall down a flight of stairs. It took me a while to accept my condition and I suffered depression for years due to this. I find writing helps me overcome the anxiety and lows my condition brings with it. Elvis Aaron Presley was another idol of mine and still is. I'm sure his lyrics inspired some of my first poetry. I'd like to thank my friend Lorna for believing in me to have my writings published , Meek, my publisher for also seeing potential in me and my daughter Shirley for helping lift my writings from the website they were on.

Acknowledgements –

Thanks to my beautiful daughter Shirley, to my friend Lorna, and to Meek, for their belief in me, and their giving me the strength to complete this book.

Katrina,
March 2020.

– Notes –

Printed in Great Britain
by Amazon